Federal Protectors

FBI

MARTY GITLIN

BLACK
RABBIT
BOOKS

Bolt is published by Black Rabbit Books
P.O. Box 227, Mankato, Minnesota 56002
www.blackrabbitbooks.com
Copyright © 2024 Black Rabbit Books

Alissa Thielges, editor; Michael Sellner, designer
and photo researcher

Library of Congress Cataloging-in-Publication Data
Names: Gitlin, Marty, author.
Title: FBI / Marty Gitlin.
Description: Mankato, Minnesota: Black Rabbit Books, [2024] |
Series: Federal protectors | Includes bibliographical references and index. |
Audience: Ages 8–12 | Audience: Grades 4–6 |
Summary: "Secret investigations and tracking down criminals are just the
beginning of what members of the FBI do. Find out what FBI agents do to keep
the United States safe"—Provided by publisher.
Identifiers: LCCN 2022031091 (print) | LCCN 2022031092 (ebook) |
ISBN 9781623106171 (library binding) | ISBN 9781623106232 (ebook)
Subjects: LCSH: United States. Federal Bureau of Investigation—Juvenile literature.
| Criminal investigation—United States—Juvenile literature.
Classification: LCC HV8144.F43 G58 2023 (print) | LCC HV8144.F43 (ebook) |
DDC 363.250973—dc23/eng/20220909
LC record available at https://lccn.loc.gov/2022031091
LC ebook record available at https://lccn.loc.gov/2022031092

Printed in China

CONTENTS

CHAPTER 1

On the

It was July 22, 1934, in Gary, Indiana. The target was John Dillinger, • • • a dangerous bank robber. He had killed 10 men. The Federal Bureau of Investigation (FBI) was on the case. They had tracked him for more than a year.

That night, the FBI got a tip. The **suspect** was going to a movie. They followed him there.

WANTED

Bank Robbery - Escape - Murde

$5000.00 REWARI

JOHN DILLINGE

DEAD OR ALIVE

Watching and Waiting

The agents waited for Dillinger outside. When he left the theater, one agent lit a cigar. It was a signal. The agents all moved closer.

Dillinger saw them. He grabbed a gun from his pants. He ran toward an alley. The FBI chased and shot him. Three bullets hit Dillinger. Soon he was dead. It was a big case. The FBI agents were heroes.

FBI agents are often called "G-men." It is short for "government men."

CHAPTER 2

An IMPORTANT Job

The FBI was created in 1908. It investigates crimes. It hunts for people who break the law. The most famous FBI director was J. Edgar Hoover. He took over in 1924. Hoover stayed there for 47 years.

The FBI protects the United States from danger. It searches for spies and **terrorists**.

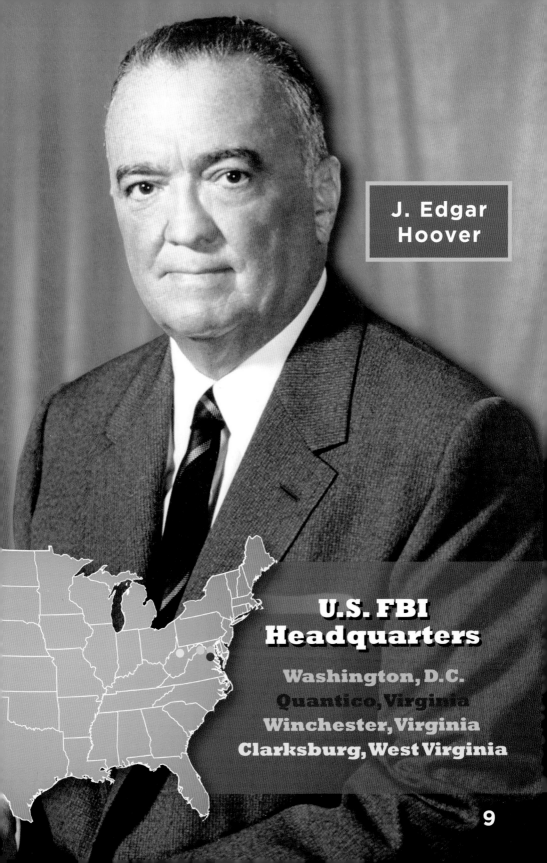

J. Edgar
Hoover

U.S. FBI Headquarters

Washington, D.C.
Quantico, Virginia
Winchester, Virginia
Clarksburg, West Virginia

Changes to the Job

The FBI has changed over the years. At first, agents didn't carry guns all the time. They could not **arrest** people. That changed in 1933. **Gang** members killed police and an FBI agent. Congress voted to allow special agents to carry guns and make arrests.

1908
FBI is created

◄· · · · · · 1924
J. Edgar Hoover becomes director, creates fingerprint program

1929 · · · ▶
FBI arrests famous gangster Al Capone

1932
First FBI crime lab opens

1946
FBI has fingerprints of 100 million people

◄·······**1963**
President John F. Kennedy is shot;
FBI investigates

1964·····►
FBI case speeds passing
of **Civil Rights** Act

1972
FBI Academy opens

1983
Hostage Rescue Team is created

◄·······**2001**
FBI focuses on terrorist attacks

Working with the FBI

Police work with the FBI. They solve crimes together. The FBI works with businesses and schools too. It has **task forces** for young people. One is the Violent Gang Task Force. Another is Junior Special Agents. Both help kids avoid drugs and gangs.

Junior Special Agents

FBI TEAMS

specialize in

hostage rescue

weapons and strategies (SWAT)

helicopter flying

16

Special Teams

When there is a **crisis**, special FBI agents respond. They have extra training. They are called in to rescue hostages. They know how to handle weapons that cause a lot of damage, like bombs. They are ready to react 24/7 to extreme situations.

Joining the

Special agents are the most famous FBI workers. But the FBI is filled with people who help find bad guys. Some people study **data** to help solve crimes. Others are business and legal experts. The FBI also hires people who work with the police.

FBI detectives work with local or state law enforcement. Special agents work with the U.S. government on federal crimes.

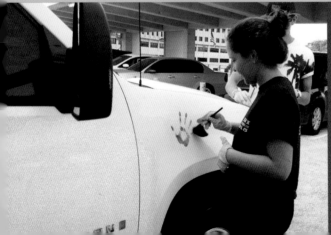

The FBI hosts a
Teen Academy
every summer.

Education and Training

All FBI agents need a college degree. Many also have a master's degree. Trainees are 23 to 36 years old. They go through two rounds of testing. There is also a fitness test.

Once they are accepted, agents report to the FBI Academy. There they have 16 weeks of classes. They train for their work in the field. Agents often work 50 hours a week.

Taking the

RIGHT STEPS

It is not easy to become an FBI agent.

Thousands apply, but only the best make it.

The steps can take a year or more to complete.

1. Apply to become an agent

2. Phase I Test: writing exam and interview

3. Meet and Greet Session

6. Conditional offer; must pass background check and graduate from the FBI Academy before getting hired

7. Medical and background checks

8. Second fitness test

9. Attend the FBI Academy

10. Be assigned to one of the 56 field offices in the U.S.

FBI AGENT

One in five FBI special agents are women.

Special Agents

Special agents usually speak a second language. They may interview people from other countries. Some are experts on computers. Some can track codes created by those who hack computers. Special agents have many talents that help solve crimes.

CHAPTER 4

Special

A tragic murder happened in 1964. Three men were killed in Mississippi. The men were fighting for voting rights for black people. The FBI took the case. • • • They quickly arrested 21 men involved. The case sped the passing of the Civil Rights Act. The FBI now has the power to look into civil rights crimes.

ISSING CALL FBI

REW GOODMAN   JAMES EARL CHANEY   MICHAEL HENRY SCHWERNER

Terror Attacks

On September 11, 2001, terrorists attacked New York City. Many people were killed. Stopping future attacks became the FBI's number one goal.

The FBI is a strong force. It investigates the most serious threats to the nation. It works with police to catch dangerous criminals. The FBI keeps Americans safe every day.

arrest (UH-rest)—to stop and hold someone by the power of the law

civil rights (SIV-il RITES)—the rights of people to have equality, no matter their race, religion, or gender

crisis (KRY-siss)—a difficult or dangerous situation that needs serious attention

gang (GANG)—a group of young people who do illegal things together and often fight other gangs

suspect (SUHS-pekt)—someone who is thought to have done a crime

task force (TASK FORSS)—a group of people specially organized for a certain job

terrorist (TER-er-ist)—someone who uses violence or threats to frighten people into obeying

BOOKS

Gish, Ashley. *FBI Hostage Rescue Team.* Mankato, Minn.: Creative Education, 2021.

Hamilton, John. *FBI.* Minneapolis: Abdo Publishing, 2022.

Sampathkumar, Mythili. *Inside the FBI.* New York: Enslow Publishing, 2019.

WEBSITES

Becoming an Agent: Preparing for the Field
www.fbi.gov/video-repository/becoming-an-agent-series-preparing-for-the-field.mp4/view

Federal Bureau of Investigation Facts for Kids
kids.kiddle.co/Federal_Bureau_of_Investigation

Future Agents in Training (FAIT) Teen Academy
www.lc.edu/FAITacademy/

INDEX